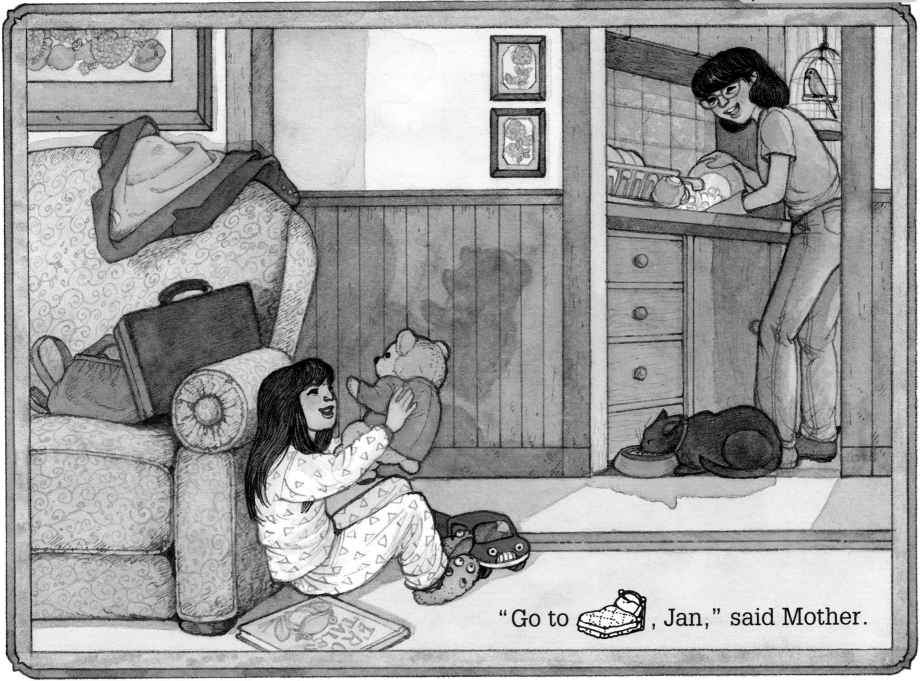

"Go to 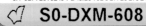, Jan," said Mother.

1

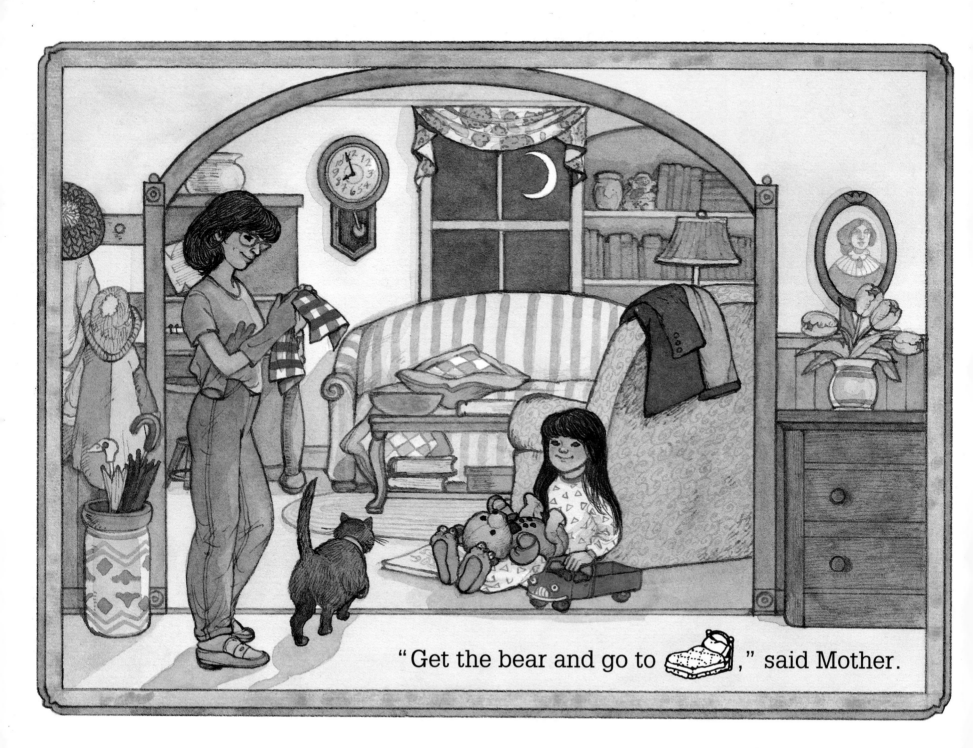

"Get the bear and go to 👟," said Mother.

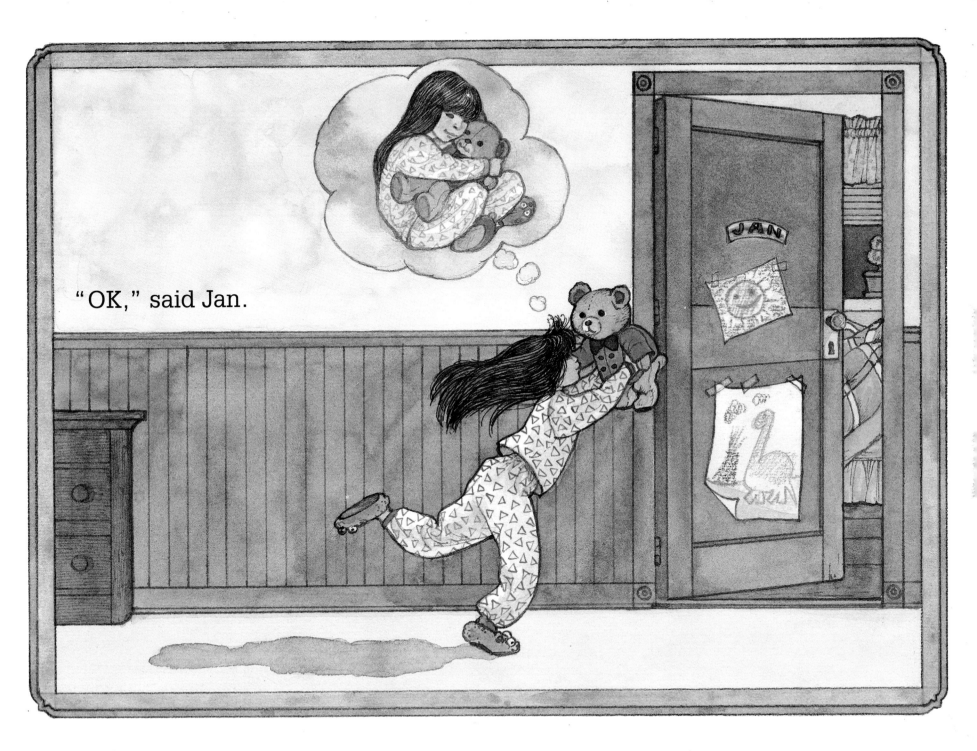

"OK," said Jan.

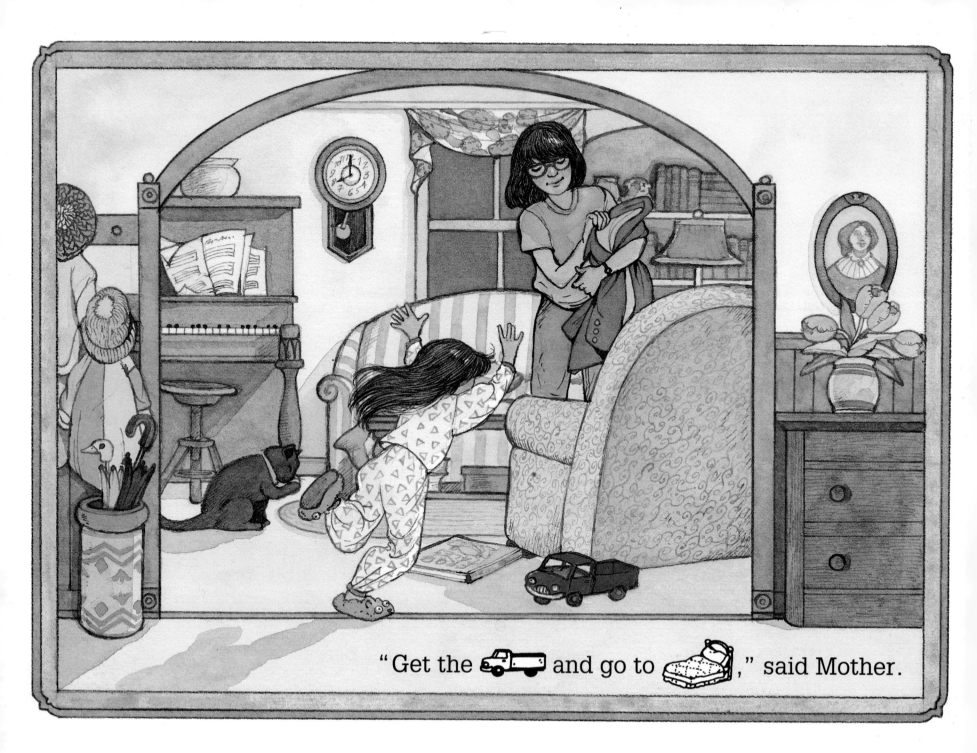

"Get the  and go to ," said Mother.

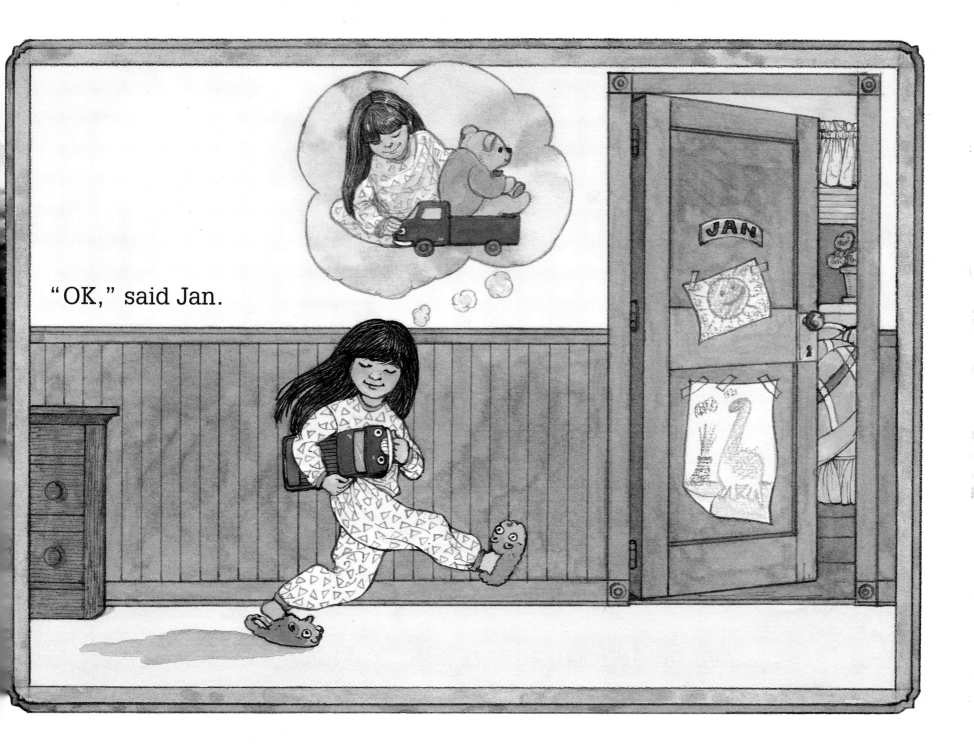

"OK," said Jan.

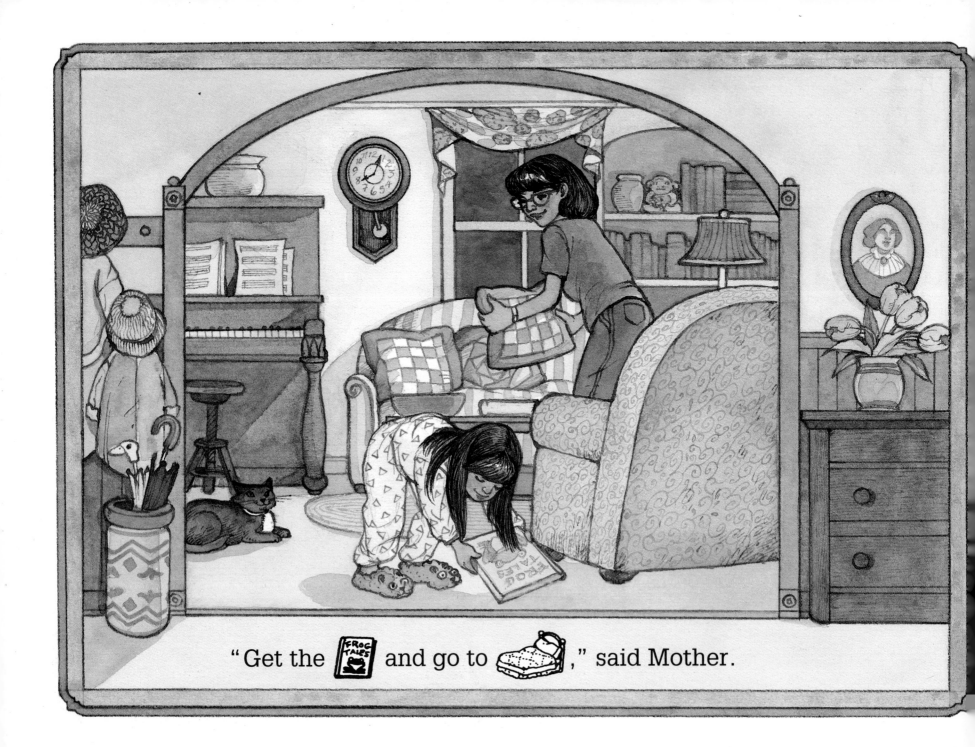

"Get the 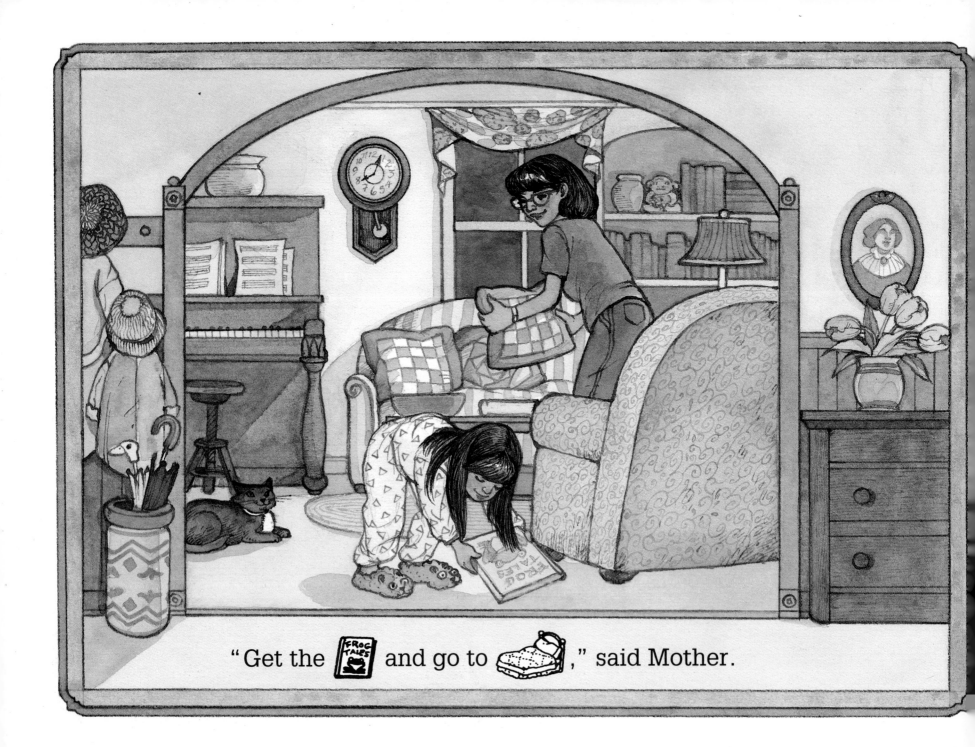 and go to 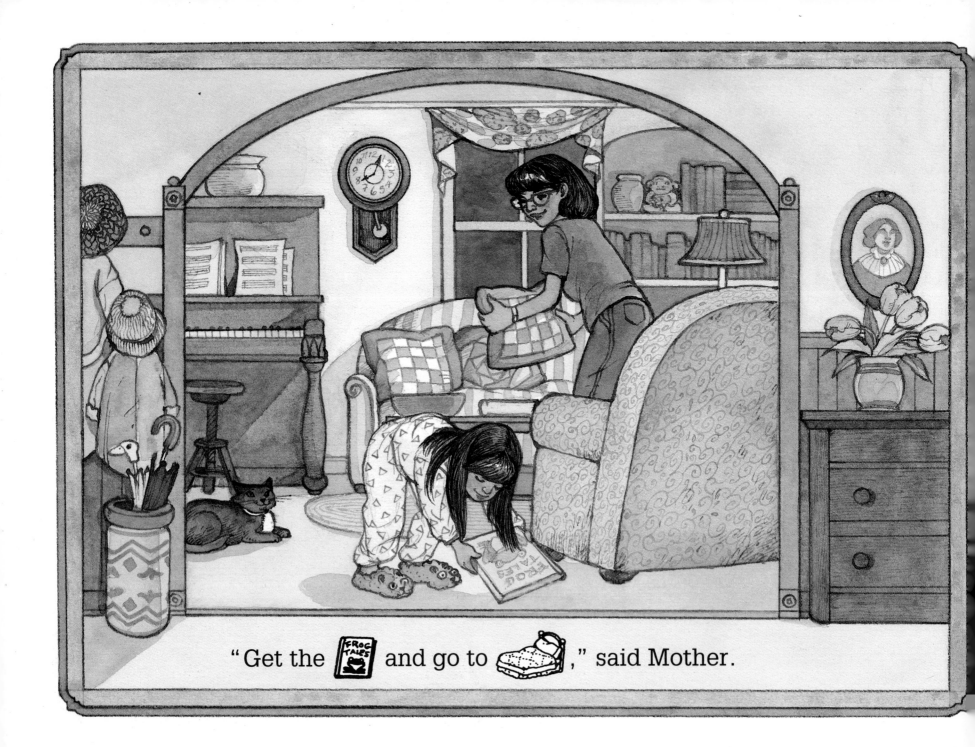," said Mother.

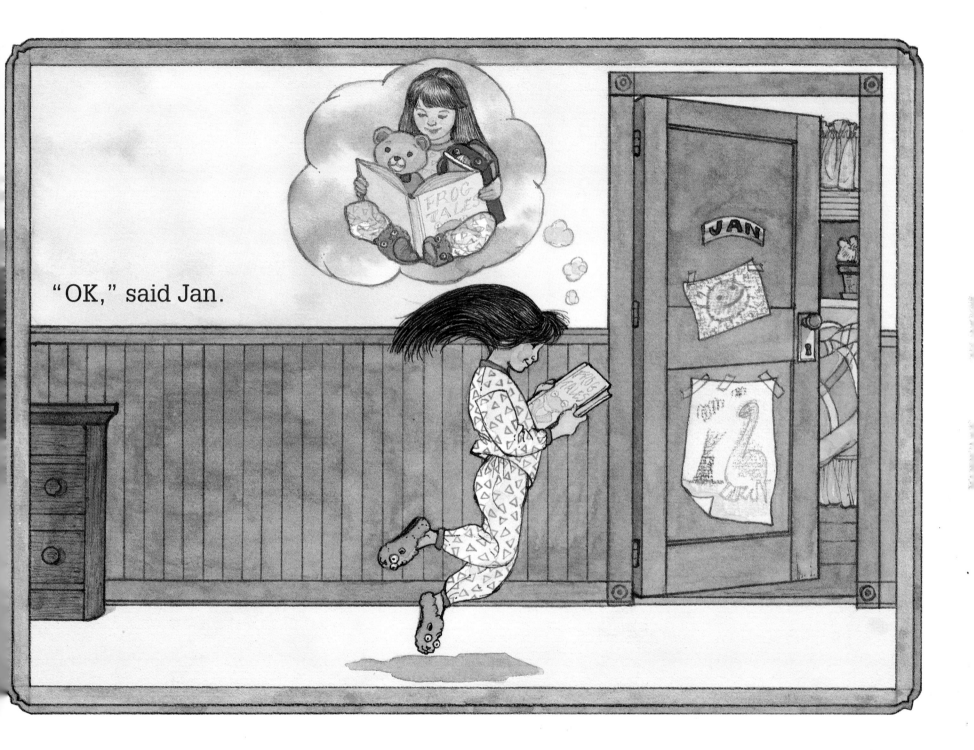

"OK," said Jan.

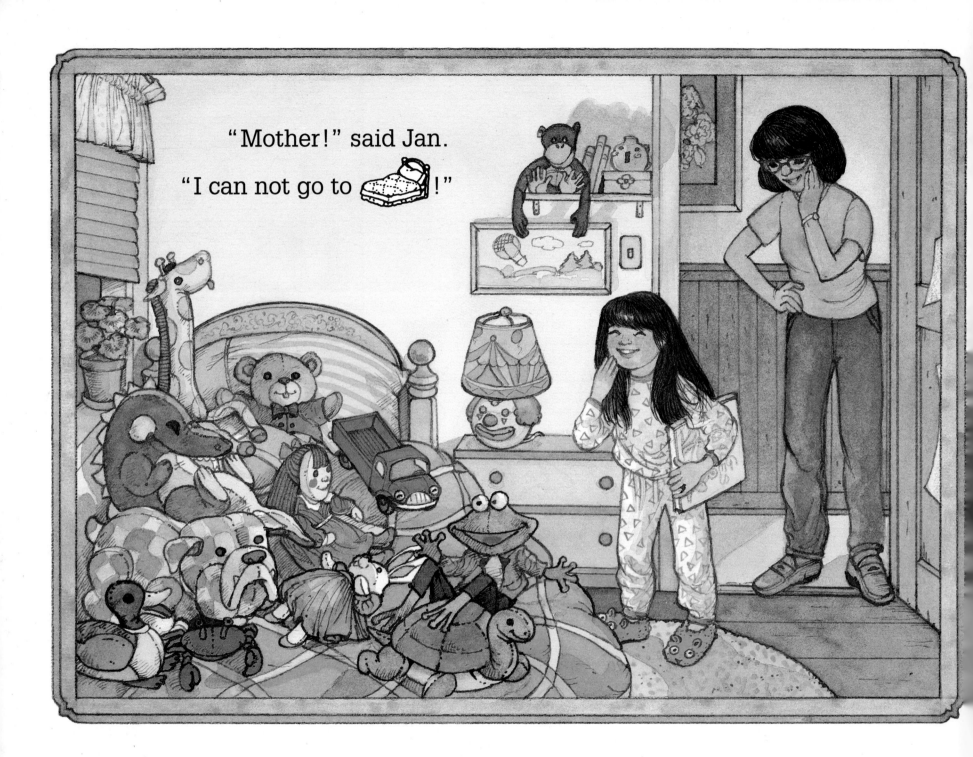

"Mother!" said Jan.

"I can not go to 👟!"